WE ARE MOVING

BY MERCER MAYER

To Julian and Gus Zuniga

HARPER FESTIVAL

An Imprint of HarperCollinsPublishers

Copyright © 2012 Mercer Mayer. All rights reserved. LITTLE CRITTER, MERCER MAYER'S LITTLE CRITTER, and MERCER MAYER'S LITTLE CRITTER
and logo are registered trademarks of Orchard House Licensing Company.

Manufactured in China.

For information address HarperCollins Children's Books, a division of HarperCollins Publishers, 10 East 53rd Street, New York, NY 10022.

Library of Congress catalog card number: 2012934238

ISBN 978-0-06-147803-1

12 13 14 15 16   SCP   10 9 8 7 6 5 4 3 2 1   ❖   First Edition

 A Big Tuna Trading Company, LLC/J.R. Sansevere Book
www.harpercollinschildrens.com   www.littlecritter.com

Mom and Dad said, "We have some exciting news."
I thought they meant we were getting a new dog.
Little Sister asked, "A new baby?"

"No," they said. "We are moving to a new house."

"That is horrible news!" I said.
Little Sister screamed and ran to her room.

At dinner Mom and Dad tried to cheer us up.
It didn't work.

I will miss my room.

The backyard will not be the same. Where will we put the rope swing and the sandbox?

I wonder, can I take my tree house?

I will have different and strange neighbors.
They might even be monsters.

Maybe there won't be any of my friends nearby.
I will have to take a bus, a train, and a boat to
see them.

What if I have to go to a new school full of bullies and a really mean teacher? "Oh no," I think.

Mom and Dad began cleaning out the house and garage. I found some really neat stuff. Mom won't let me keep any of it.

Mom said, "The Friendly Helping Critters are coming by to pick it all up. Now leave it alone."

My friends came over to keep me company.

But we were just too sad to play.

Finally, moving day arrived.
A big truck came to our house.
It had big tires.

The movers began to move all of the furniture into the big truck.

But I wouldn't let them touch my stuff.

Dad said I had to. I kept my small stuffed bear.

Everything was packed in the truck.
It was time to leave. I didn't want to go.

Dad had to carry me to the car.

We drove into the driveway of the new house.
It was even near my school.

All my friends were waiting in front
when we drove up.

The house and yard are great.
Sometimes moving is not so bad, after all.